Is It OK If This Monster Stays For Lunch?

Story By
Martyn Godfrey

Pictures By
Susan Wilkinson

TORONTO   OXFORD   NEW YORK
OXFORD UNIVERSITY PRESS

To my good friend Frank O'Keeffe,
thanks for making me laugh.
— M.G.

To my husband and three children,
whose support created an artist.
— S.W.

Oxford University Press, 70 Wynford Drive, Don Mills, Ontario, M3C 1J9
Toronto Oxford New York Delhi Bombay Calcutta Madras Karachi
Kuala Lumpur Singapore Hong Kong Tokyo Nairobi Dar es Salaam
Cape Town Melbourne Auckland Madrid

and associated companies
Berlin Ibadan

Canadian Cataloguing in Publication Data

Godfrey, Martyn
Is it ok if this monster stays for lunch?

ISBN 0-19-540882-9 (pbk.)

I. Wilkinson, Susan. II. Title.

PS8563.03I7 1992   jC813'.54   C91-094752-X
PZ7.G64Is 1992

Text © Martyn Godfrey, 1992
Illustrations © Susan Wilkinson, 1992

Oxford is a trademark of Oxford University Press

3 4 - 5 4 3

Printed in Hong Kong

I'm lucky.

I live next to the playground. It has swings and slides and old tires and sand and monkey bars and teeter-totters and a rocket ship. All sorts of weird things like to play there.

On **Monday,** when I was monkeying around on the monkey bars, I met a monster named Monty.

Monty was mauve and mouldy and a little mangy. He had short, sharp teeth, elegant eyes, green, bumpy skin and hairy ears. And Monty wore his clothes inside out so you could see the labels which tell you how to wash them.

Monty was nicer than most of the monsters I've met monkeying around on a **Monday,** so I asked him to come to my house for lunch.

Mom was sitting at the kitchen table adding up numbers because she's a bank manager and brings home lots of numbers.

"Hi, Mom. It's me, Megan."

"Mmmm," Mom mmmmed.

"Is it OK if this monster stays for lunch?"

Mom kept adding. "What an imagination you have, Megan. Monsters can't stay for lunch."

On **Tuesday,** I was playing with my dump truck in the sand when I met Denise Dinosaur.

Denise was dappled and dozy and her skin was scaly and scrumpled and she had big, bulgy, bloodshot eyes and glasses that kept slipping down her slopey nose.

She giggled all the time as if everything I said was funny.

Denise was the nicest dinosaur I'd ever met while trucking on a **Tuesday,** so I invited her home for lunch.

Dad was sitting at the kitchen table reading a book because he works at a library and brings lots of books home.

"Hi, Dad. It's your darling daughter."

"Hmmm," Dad hmmmed.

"This is Denise Dinosaur, Dad. Can she stay for lunch?"

Dad shook his head and kept reading. "How do you think up such silly things? Dinosaurs definitely don't stay for lunch."

On **Wednesday,** I was swinging and singing a silly song when
I met a space creature, Sissy from Saturn.

Sissy was pale and pink and a little plump. She had four furry, floppy feet and eager egg-shaped eyes. When Sissy joined in my song, her body jiggled and juggled like jelly and she hissed through her teeth which made me shiver.

I'd never met a space creature quite as nice as Sissy while swinging on a **Wednesday,** so I asked her to come to my house for lunch.

My older brother, Allen, was at the kitchen table checking parts of his motorbike and mumbling the words that Mom and Dad don't let me say.

"Hi, Allen. This is Sissy from Saturn. I want her to stay for lunch."

"Give me a break, kid," Allen said. "Aliens can't stay for lunch."

On **Thursday,** at the teeter-totter, I met a troll named Tammy.

Tammy was terribly tiny and wore a torn, tattered, too-tight T-shirt. She had a black boot with a buckle on one foot and a blue boot with a bell on the other. She kept a slimy pet slug named Sloopy in the pocket of her purple, polka-dot pants.

Tammy was by far the nicest troll I'd met while teeter-tottering on a **Thursday,** so I invited her to lunch.

My other brother, Steven, was sitting at the kitchen table sorting through his baseball cards. Steven thinks he's all grown up, even though he's only eleven.

"Hi, Steven. It's me."

"Hi," Steven snapped.

"This terrific troll is Tammy. Can she stay for lunch?"

"Don't be stupid," Steven snarled. "There's no such thing as a stupid troll. And even if there was, it certainly couldn't stay for stupid lunch."

On **Friday,** Graham Gremlin played rocket ship with me.

Graham was grey and grimy and really quite grungy. He blew big bubbles of blueberry bubble gum and he told funny jokes like, "Why did the chicken cross the playground?"

"Why?" I wondered.

"To get to the other slide." And we both laughed long and loud like loons.

PARK

"You're the nicest person I've ever rocketed with on a **Friday,**" Graham told me. "Would you like to come to my house for lunch?"

"I can't," I said. "I'm not allowed to go where someone in my family can't see me. Why don't you come with me?"

Grandma and Grampa were sitting at the kitchen table looking grumpy. They were grumbling about something in the newspaper.

"Is it OK, Grandma and Grampa, if this gremlin called Graham stays for lunch?"

"Our stocks are down," Grandma and Grampa grumped together. "Don't bother us right now. Gremlins may not stay for lunch."

On **Saturday** it rained, so I couldn't go outside. Instead, I sat by the window and watched the dragons dance daintily and delicately in the playground. Dragons don't mind dancing in a downpour, especially on a **Saturday.**

On **Sunday,** while paddling in a puddle, I met Michael.

Michael had black, curly hair and a wide smile which showed his missing front teeth. He wore a red shirt that said ''Super-Kid'' and blue jeans and bright red sneakers. We played tag until we were both out of breath.

Then Steven called from our house.
"Hey, Megan! It's time for stupid lunch."

"Who's that?" asked Michael.

"Only Steven," I said. "You're the nicest kid I've paddled with here
on a **Sunday.** Do you want to eat lunch with me?"

"Hi, everyone," I said. "This is my friend, Michael. Can he stay for lunch?"

"Of course," Mom said.

"Great," I grinned. "But how come Michael can stay when Monty Monster, Denise Dinosaur, Sissy from Saturn, Tammy Troll and Graham Gremlin couldn't?"

Mom looked at Dad. Allen looked at Steven. Grandma looked at Grampa.

''That's because...er...that's because...um...'' Dad said.
''That's because...Michael is your friend.''

"But they were my friends, too."

"You should have told us," Mom said. "Friends can stay for lunch."

I ran to the back door and yelled across to the playground.

And that was the finest, funniest, friendliest lunch we've ever shared on a **Sunday.**